Who ate all the pies?

C. B. Lindsay

For Stuart – who prefers his
Mum's rice pudding

First published in Great Britain in 2010 by
TickTock Entertainment Ltd, The Old Sawmill,
103 Goods Station Road, Tunbridge Wells, Kent, TN1 2DP

This edition and artwork © 2010 *TickTock* Entertainment Ltd
Text © 2010 C. B. Lindsay

ISBN-13: 978-1-84898-266-6 pbk

A CIP catalogue record for this book is available
from the British Library.

Printed in Great Britain

1 3 5 7 9 8 6 4 2

Who ate all the pies?

Chapters

The pie's the limit

"More pies!" belched Cuthbert, spraying crumbs everywhere.

"There are another six on the way, dear," Granny said, panting as she knelt down to open the oven door. "You're going to pass your record if you keep this up."

"Don't care, need more custard pies!"

"I just hope you don't turn yellow again," Granny mumbled into her apron as a cloud of sweet-smelling steam rose out of the oven.

"Custard pies! Custard pies!" begged Cuthbert, drooling onto the table.

"Just a moment, Cuthbops." Granny mopped her brow with a custard-covered

oven mitt, smearing a yellow streak across her forehead. With a great deal of effort, she hobbled to her feet, balancing a tray of pies in each hand and another on top of her head.

"We'll just leave these to cool over here. Shouldn't take long," Granny said cautiously as she shuffled towards the windowsill.

"GIVE ME PIES!"

"There you are then," she sighed, shovelling pies onto the large silver platter before Cuthbert. "Careful — they're still hot."

Cuthbert grabbed the biggest of the custard pies and shoved a spoonful into

slurp, slurp
chomp

his mouth. Custard ran down Cuthbert's arms and dripped all over his school shirt as he guzzled one pie after another.

"Nyom, nyom, slurp, slurp, chomp, chomp, chomp."

"Granny needs a little sit-down now, dear," said Granny, edging towards the kitchen door. "But don't worry. I'll make you some more pies for supper."

For as long as Cuthbert had lived with Granny, mealtimes had always been the same. Granny's custard pies had become the centre of Cuthbert's world since his parents were killed in a tragic salsa dancing accident five years earlier.

As a result of his extraordinary intake of custard pies, Cuthbert had developed quite an impressive pot-belly.

"You're just big-boned," Granny would say when Cuthbert told her how some of the children at school teased him. "Pay no attention to the scrawny brats!"

Every day after school, Cuthbert would follow the sweet custardy smell that led all the way to Granny's kitchen. There, he'd squeeze into his favourite chair and watch wide-eyed as Granny lifted the first batch of golden pies off the windowsill and plonked them down on

his special platter. As he scoffed his way through these, there would always be more baking in the oven.

But one fateful day, everything changed... As Cuthbert walked home from school, he sensed that something wasn't quite right. First, he took a wrong turn down Pudding Lane. Then, while taking a shortcut back to his regular route, he tripped over an abandoned saucepan in a grotty alley.

"What on earth is the matter with me today?" Cuthbert exclaimed in total bewilderment.

Suddenly, it dawned on him. "I can't smell custard pies!" Since leaving school he hadn't picked up on the scent at all.

As he rejoined Crumbly Way, Cuthbert's worst fears were confirmed. There was an unmistakable absence of the syrupy smell that led straight to Granny's kitchen table.

By the time he arrived home, Cuthbert had concluded that Granny was suffering

from some sort of illness, like weevil-knee or the mange. It had to be serious. Nothing had ever stopped her from making custard pies before.

"Are you unwell, Granny?" he hollered up the stairs, assuming she had gone to bed to recover.

"I am perfectly well, Cuthbert. Would you like a slice of turnip?"

Cuthbert was shocked to hear Granny's croaky voice coming from the kitchen. Entering the room, he wedged himself into his chair and watched Granny feverishly chopping up a turnip.

"Where are all the custard pies?" Cuthbert asked, aghast.

Granny gave a little jump, causing the piece of turnip she was slicing to ricochet off the window and lodge itself in her left ear.

"Lovely bit of turnip. Good for the bowels, that's what I say," Granny stammered as she dislodged the piece of turnip from her ear and dropped it into a bowl with the rest of the slices.

"Turnip? I'm not eating turnip! Where are all my pies?" Cuthbert demanded.

"Did I ever tell you about the time I came second in a baby-rolling competition in 1942? I rolled your Uncle Bernard."

Cuthbert thought for a moment. "No. And that's not the point, Granny! Why haven't you baked me any pies?"

"I was cheated out of first place, you know. Betty Shingles doused her baby in butter and it shot down that mountain like lightning."

"GRANNY – I WANT MY PIES NOW!"

"I shouldn't complain really, that baby was so slippery no one was able to catch it."

By now Cuthbert had become very confused. "What is going on, Granny?" he whimpered.

Granny didn't answer his question,

but continued to recall the events of the 1942 Baby-Rolling Contest loudly.

"There you go, Cuthbert," said Granny, eventually catching her breath as she dolloped a huge mound of mashed turnip onto his platter.

Cuthbert gawped at the orangey-brown substance and then looked up at Granny pleadingly.

"Well dear, I can't hang around chatting all day," she said, avoiding his gaze. And with that, she flung off her apron and darted out of the kitchen.

Cuthbert sat open-mouthed with shock. He sat this way for quite some time until his tummy began to rumble.

"I can't believe I'm going to do this," he groaned. Then he lifted his spoon and reluctantly began to eat the mashed turnip.

Shake a leg, foot, arm...

In the school playground the next day, the effects of having gone so long without a single custard pie began to show on Cuthbert. It started as a slight trembling in his fingers, then spread to his arms, down his back, through his legs and into his toes until it became a fully fledged case of the all-over body-shakes. Not wanting to draw attention to himself, Cuthbert attempted to blend into a crowd that had gathered around the school bully, Morris Macaroon.

"Wh-wh-whatzzz go-go-going on?" Cuthbert stuttered to the girl standing next to him.

"Well, Arnold Ankles was playing

hopscotch by himself again, when Morris walked right up to him and knocked off his glasses! I think Morris is annoyed because Mrs Frilly made them Study Buddies."

Cuthbert shuffled closer to get a better look at what was going on.

"You'll never find them, Lanky Ankie!" Morris cackled as he watched Arnold scrabbling about for his glasses.

Arnold was a weedy boy whose mousey blond hair was styled into a rather hideous bowl cut. For as long as Cuthbert had known him, Arnold had always worn a pair of orange-rimmed glasses that dwarfed most of his face, but these were now lying several feet away.

"Did you know your ears stick out?" Morris taunted. "From here they look like satellite dishes! Has Mad Ankles been experimenting on you?"

The younger children who were listening let out a collective "Ooooohhh" when Morris said the name Mad Ankles.

"Maybe he'll experiment on your brain next and then you won't be so smart, will you, Lanky Ankie?"

"Leave my dad alone," said Arnold in a trembling voice.

There was a deep intake of breath from the crowd.

"Who gave you permission to talk?" Morris demanded. "Right, that's it. I'm just going to have to drop-kick you."

Cuthbert, who by this point had juddered his way to the front of the crowd, was now shaking so violently that his arm suddenly flung out and jabbed Morris right in the eye.

"Ahh!" Morris screeched. "I'm going to tell my mum on you!" Cuthbert took one look at the blubbering school bully and scarpered.

He ran as fast as he could, but didn't get very far. Panting and shaking, he sat down at the edge of the playground to catch his breath.

This is just great, he thought, feeling sorry for himself. *No pies and now the shakes!* Just then, Cuthbert spotted a bright -yellow shape walking towards him. As the shape got closer, it began to come into focus: it was a huge custard pie! But this pie was unlike any he had seen before – it had arms and legs! Cuthbert could feel the saliva running down his chin.

Funny, he thought, *I've never seen a custard pie with legs before. Although it has been a while since I saw one...* The giant custard pie was now standing right in front of him, so he leaned forward and bit into it.

"Ouch!"

Cuthbert looked up, quite sure that custard pies did not shout. It was then that he realised that he had just bitten Arnold Ankles.

"I'm sorry, I thought you were a giant custard pie," Cuthbert said disappointedly.

"Well I'm not a custard pie," Arnold replied cautiously, "although Dad sometimes thinks I'm a touring Swedish trapeze artist."

Cuthbert had never met Arnold's scientist father, but everyone knew he was as mad as a toothbrush.

"You got your glasses back, then?" Cuthbert said, swiftly changing the subject.

"Yes, but I probably wouldn't have if you hadn't saved me like that! Thanks, Cuthbert!"

"I didn't mean to save you. I've got the shakes," Cuthbert quivered.

"Oh," said Arnold disappointedly. "Are you walking home today?"

"Yes," Cuthbert reluctantly admitted. Although Arnold lived very close to Granny's house, Cuthbert had always avoided him. It was bad enough getting teased for being 'big-boned'. He didn't want to be made fun of for being friends with Mad Ankles' weird son too.

"I know!" Arnold said excitedly. "Why don't I walk with you? We can get some sweets from my house – Dad says that sweets cure most ailments."

Cuthbert tried to think of an excuse,

but the more he thought, the harder he shook. And the harder he shook, the more tempting Arnold's offer became. So at half-past three that afternoon, Cuthbert found himself juddering towards Mad Ankles' house, led by a jubilant Arnold.

Don't fight the fridge that feeds you

"Dad! I'm home!" Arnold shouted. "My friend from school is here too and he's got the sh—" Arnold trailed off as he stood transfixed in the living room.

This is it, Cuthbert thought, *I'm about to become Mad Ankles' next guinea pig!* Plucking up the courage to look over Arnold's shoulder, Cuthbert was relieved to see nothing out of the ordinary other than a terrible mess. Upturned chairs, wonky picture frames and various other household items lay at random angles across the floor.

"DAD!" Arnold yelled.

"What seems to be the problem, Arnie?" said a voice from behind them, making Cuthbert jump.

"Look at the state of the place, Dad!"

"Ah, that. Well, a few things do seem to have been misplaced. All easily amended, young Arnold." Mad Ankles gazed over their heads at the untidy living room.

It was the first time Cuthbert had seen Arnold's dad up close, and he noticed with curiosity that Mad Ankles was wearing the same glasses as his son (only bigger). His hair sat like an untameable bush on top of his head and his features were arranged in a way that made him look permanently dazed.

"Dad, this is Cuthbert, my friend from school," Arnold said, beaming from ear to ear. Cuthbert was stunned to be described as Arnold's friend. He hardly knew him!

"Ah yes – you live with Granny, don't you? I've seen you in the neighbourhood. It's nice to finally meet you. As you probably already know, I'm Professor Ankles," Arnold's father declared, shaking Cuthbert's hand rather vigorously. For such a feeble-looking man, Professor Ankles had quite a firm handshake.

"You appear to have a bad case of the shakes, young man. Here, have a sweet." He smiled as he produced a fluff-covered strawberry sherbet from deep within the pocket of his lab coat.

"Th-th-thanks," Cuthbert stuttered as

he reluctantly popped the sweet into his mouth. "Mmmm, nice," he forced himself to say while trying not to touch the fluffy bits with his tongue. Surprisingly, his shakes started to subside.

"What's for dinner tonight, Dad? Can Cuthbert stay?" Arnold pleaded.

But Professor Ankles didn't seem to be listening. He was frozen to the spot and staring straight into the kitchen. Grabbing the first thing that came to hand – which happened to be an umbrella – he whispered, "Keep still, boys, and don't say a word!" Then, without warning, he ran into the kitchen, umbrella poised for battle, shouting, "There's no escape this time, you rogue!"

There was a loud bang followed by a series of cracking noises. Arnold and Cuthbert exchanged fearful looks.

"Should we go in?" Cuthbert shouted over the din.

"You go first," Arnold cowered.

Peering round the kitchen door, Cuthbert was met by a most peculiar sight. Professor Ankles had tipped over the fridge and was whacking it with the umbrella.

"You'll never run off on me again!" Professor Ankles barked as he hit the fridge over and over again.

Cuthbert cleared his throat loudly.

"Get back, Cuthbert!" Professor Ankles yelled. It was then that Cuthbert saw how Mad Ankles had got his nickname. The Professor's eyes bulged out, his nostrils

flared and his glasses were positioned diagonally across his face.

"Um... why are you beating your fridge, Mad— I mean, Professor Ankles?" he enquired in as casual a tone as he could muster.

Professor Ankles stopped whacking the fridge and looked down at it with a puzzled expression. Scratching his head, he knelt down and pulled open the fridge door. The contents spilled forth all over the floor.

"Oh dear," Professor Ankles said quietly, "I thought... " There was a long pause.

"What did you think?" said Cuthbert, wanting to understand. But Professor Ankles had already scuttled out of the kitchen, muttering to himself.

"Dad, what *is* going on?" Arnold called after him.

No use crying over spilt custard

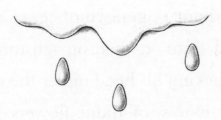

Cuthbert looked up at the sky. It was beginning to rain. But this wasn't your typical rain. This was bright-yellow custard rain and it was landing with loud splats all over Cuthbert! Just then, Arnold and Professor Ankles appeared in front of him holding matching umbrellas and began to tap-dance through the puddles of custard that were forming on the ground. As he watched their extraordinary performance, Cuthbert climbed into a nearby custard-filled bath. Sticking his head under the surface, he saw a row of giant flowers singing *Sing A Song of Sixpence*.

Cuthbert awoke with a jolt. His brow was soaked with sweat and the song from his dream rang distantly in his ears. The smell of something sweet filled his nostrils. Could his senses be fooling him yet again? He closed his eyes, but he could still smell the syrupy goodness of...

"Custard pies!" he cried, jumping out of bed. Glancing at his bedside clock, he frowned. "But it's after midnight! What's going on?"

Unable to fight his curiosity, Cuthbert resolved to seek out the source of the aroma no matter how late it was. Sneaking as quietly as he could down the stairs, Cuthbert followed his nose towards the kitchen. The door was shut, but golden light filtered underneath. Kneeling down, he peered through the keyhole.

The room was so full of steam that he thought for a moment that Granny had taken up smoking cigars again. As the steam began to clear he could just make out Granny poised over the stove.

Four huge pots sat bubbling and boiling over with hot yellow liquid. Cuthbert knew this was the real thing – rich, creamy, satisfying custard!

Granny seemed to be in a hurry. Her perm had become so saturated with steam that it had transformed into a trendy bob. It took quite an effort for tiny Granny to lift the massive pots down from the stove and pour their contents into the pastry crusts that had been cooking in the oven. Her hands were trembling so much that custard splattered all over her apron and onto the floor. Oblivious to the mess around her, Granny scooped out the finished pies, arranged them in a tartan trolley bag and solemnly wheeled them out the back door.

Cuthbert waddled into the kitchen, his hands greedily grasping for leftovers. In his excitement, his right foot slipped on a puddle of custard, sending him skidding across the floor.

"YIKES!" Almost toppling over, Cuthbert grabbed the pink flamingo tapestry hanging next to the window.

"Keep quiet!" he told himself, aware that Granny could be using her Super Ear 5000 hearing aid, which had got him into trouble before.

Cuthbert gazed out into the darkness. He could just make out Granny trundling her trolley bag down the garden path towards the old shed. When she reached the rickety steps, she pulled down one stocking and produced a key.

That's strange, Cuthbert thought, *the old*

shed has never been locked before. Why on earth is Granny sneaking in? Cuthbert had never liked the garden shed; it was full of dust and cobwebs that made him sneeze.

After a moment's pause, Granny pushed open the shed door and dragged in the trolley bag of custard pies. Just before she shut the door, Cuthbert heard her say faintly, "H-h-here are your pies."

Astonished and shivering (he feared a return of the shakes), Cuthbert turned away. It was clear that this batch of custard pies would never see the inside of his tummy. But who *was* eating them? *Those are MY pies*, thought Cuthbert in disbelief. As he climbed back up the stairs, Cuthbert resolved to find out who – or what – Granny was visiting in the old

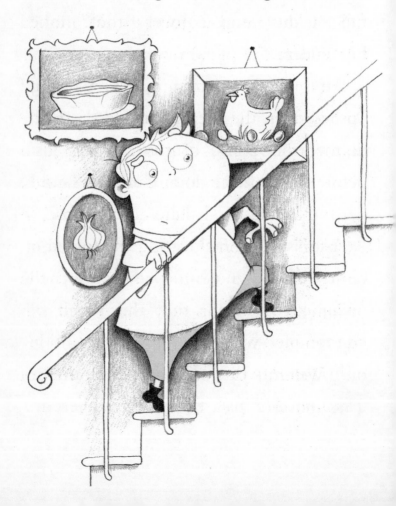

shed in the middle of the night, armed to the dentures with custard pies.

"So what are you going to do?" asked Arnold in the playground the next day.

"I think the only way to get my custard pies back is to take a trip down to the old shed tonight," Cuthbert declared, a little more bravely than he actually felt.

It had taken Cuthbert some time to explain the events of the previous night, but eventually Arnold understood the dilemma facing his new friend and was determined to help.

"Well, I won't let you go alone. I'm coming too!"

Search
every nook
and Granny

When Cuthbert opened the front door that evening, he scarcely recognised Arnold. He was wearing a safari hat and a massive pair of binoculars.

"I managed to get Dad's adventure hat and best of all... his night vision goggles!" Arnold cried excitedly.

"Great! But you mustn't let Granny see you in those goggles or she'll definitely suspect that we are up to something!"

At half-past nine, Cuthbert poured Granny a sherry.

Then another one.

Then another one.

And then one more just for luck.

Her cheeks became rosy and she began to hiccup. "It was nice to meet you – *hic!* – Arthur," she said, patting Arnold on top of his hat.

Granny then insisted on singing a few songs before she hobbled up to bed mumbling, "I'm sure I was supposed to stay awake for something."

"No, Granny," Cuthbert called after her. "*Attack of the Killer Badger Beasts* was on telly last week, remember?"

But she had already disappeared into her room.

Cuthbert and Arnold listened at Granny's door until they heard the sound of snoring.

"If we want to get into the shed, first we have to get the key," Cuthbert whispered. "And with any luck it's still in Granny's stockings."

Loosening the straps to accommodate the width of his face, Cuthbert pulled on the night-vision goggles.

"I'm going in!" he said firmly, before opening Granny's bedroom door and creeping inside.

Things slowly came into focus: a wardrobe, a chair, a pool table and

of course the
bed from which
Granny's snores
could be heard.
Where do I begin?
Cuthbert thought,
looking round the
room. *Ah-ha! The
washing basket!* Delving
in, he was immediately
hit by a revolting smell.

"Poo yuk!" Cuthbert
whispered, holding his nose
in disgust. Taking a closer
look, he saw that the
top layer of clothes

was covered in mushy orange gunk. "Turnip smoothie," Cuthbert recalled with a shudder.

Rummaging deeper, Cuthbert began to smell something much more pleasing. Instead of turnip-smeared clothes, he discovered several aprons all covered in bright-yellow custard stains. Resisting the urge to taste the clothes, he moved his search on to Granny's wardrobe. There, he found only a neat row of crisp white aprons, several power drills and the snorkel he had got Granny for Christmas.

Suddenly, Granny gave a particularly thunderous snore. Cuthbert turned to make sure she hadn't woken herself up, and saw her left leg jutting out from under the duvet – fully stockinged. *Oh dear*, Cuthbert thought. *She's still wearing them! Maybe I overdid the sherry. I'll never get the key now!*

He was just beginning to consider ways he could ram down the shed door, when he noticed a glass on Granny's bedside table. Edging closer, he saw that it contained Granny's false teeth, and clasped between the back molars was the key! Dipping his hand into the water,

Cuthbert winced as he fished about the glass attempting to prise the key from Granny's teeth. But they were sharp and cut into Cuthbert's fingers.

"Ouch!" he yelped before he could stop himself.

Granny stirred and raspily cried out, "I can't bake any more custard pies! Please have mercy on old Granny!" She then rolled over and continued snoring.

Cuthbert drew a sigh of relief and, taking extra care, managed to extract the key from the teeth.

"I heard Granny's voice. Did she wake up?" Arnold peeped as Cuthbert fled the room.

"No, she was just having a bad dream."

"I bet it was about whatever's going on in the shed," Arnold whispered.

"Yes," Cuthbert agreed. "We need to get to the bottom of this. We'll go down to the shed now – but we won't go empty-handed."

"What do you mean?" Arnold squeaked nervously.

"If whoever is in there likes pies so much, I'll bake him some that are REALLY special." It was the first time Cuthbert had ever thought of making pies himself. It would be a difficult task but someone, it seemed, had to do it.

Many utensils make light work

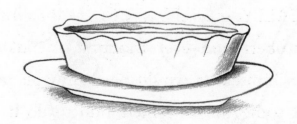

"Set aside the things that look useful for pie-making," Cuthbert instructed Arnold as they raided the kitchen cupboards. Among the equipment they gathered were an electric whisk, some pots, a mixing bowl and tongs.

"Perfect!" Cuthbert smiled as he inspected the items. "Now for the ingredients." Cuthbert had seen Granny making custard pies so many times before that he remembered what to do.

To make the pastry, he lobbed a whole tub of lard into the mixing bowl, along with flour, sugar and eggs.

"Could you pass me the whisk please, Arnold?" Cuthbert asked.

"Check," barked Arnold, passing him the whisk.

Cuthbert turned the setting to 'fast' and plunged it into the sloppy mixture.

SPLAT! Cuthbert turned to look at Arnold. His face was covered in gloop.

"You look like that swamp monster Granny was watching on television!" laughed Cuthbert.

"You look like Dad the time his earwax experiment backfired!" Arnold giggled, pointing at Cuthbert's dripping face.

Cuthbert licked his lips. "Mmmm, it tastes good, though!" he grinned. "Maybe a little bit more sugar?"

"Yes, I think you're right," Arnold agreed, licking the end of his nose.

After hours of mixing and stirring, watching and waiting, the pies were finally ready. Cuthbert opened the oven door and pulled out a batch of lopsided, slightly charred pies.

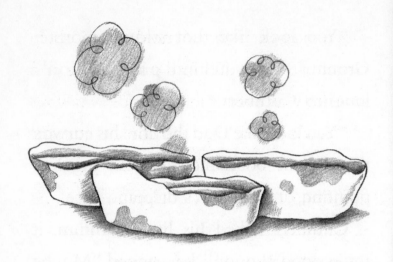

"Wow!" gasped Arnold. "They look amazing!"

"Yes, they aren't bad at all," Cuthbert said. "But they're missing something..." He hunched over the pies so that Arnold couldn't see what he was doing. Arnold feared that he might be eating them, but when Cuthbert turned around, all the pies remained. In fact, Arnold couldn't help noticing that they looked a little fuller and somehow an even brighter shade of yellow.

"You're a terribly good cook, Cuthbert! Much better than my dad."

"Thanks, Arnold. I couldn't have done it without you, you know."

Arnold beamed with delight.

Slipping out into the night air, they dragged Granny's pie-filled trolley bag behind them. As Arnold followed Cuthbert into the darkness, his teeth began to chatter with a mixture of cold and fear. When the shed came into view, Cuthbert's tummy gave a lurch and his

hands began to tremble. But these shakes weren't brought on by custard pie deprivation.

"Perhaps I'll get used to the turnip," Cuthbert grimaced.

"Now, you know that's nonsense!"

Cuthbert didn't even have to think

about it. "You're right," he
admitted, pulling the key from
his pocket. "Time to deliver our
special pies. We're going in!"

The wooden door creaked menacingly
as the key turned in its rusty lock and
swung open. It was warmer in the shed
than outside, and there was a strong
musty smell in the air.

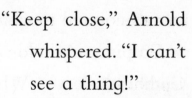

"Keep close," Arnold
whispered. "I can't
see a thing!"

Using the night-
vision goggles,
Cuthbert scanned
the shed for any

sign of life. Everything seemed normal –
a shelf holding a variety of old bottles,
the lawnmower perched on its side,
Cuthbert's old bicycle, an unusually
large, crumb-covered machine and
Granny's rusty chainsaw. Everything was
as it should be.

"Wait a second!" Cuthbert suddenly
cried. "I don't remember seeing that large
crumb-covered machine before!"

Gasping, Arnold grabbed hold of
Cuthbert's sleeve. "Where?"

But before Cuthbert could answer, the
machine gave a rattle, scattering crumbs
all over the floor, and in a deep, booming
voice it roared, "OVER HERE!"

Revenge is a dish best served HOT!

Two shutters clunked open to reveal a pair of shining red eyes.

"AARGH!" the boys yelled, shielding their faces from the powerful beams of light.

"Where is the old crone?" the machine demanded in its crunching, clanking voice.

"Sh-sh-she—um—isn't coming," Cuthbert stuttered.

"WHAT?" the jagged mouth cried, showering them both in crumbs. "Where are all the custard pies?"

"W-w-we brought you some of our own!" Arnold blurted.

The machine gave a bellowing laugh.

"You mere boys thought you could make custard pies that would satisfy me?!"

"Well, yes, actually. I'd say they're almost as exquisite as Granny's," Cuthbert said defensively.

"Very well!" the machine boomed. "They will have to suffice! Bring them to me!"

Taking the pies out of the trolley bag, Cuthbert laid them in front of the machine's steel jaws. Then he stood back and beheld the machine in all its metal glory. In some ways, it looked like an oversized cooker, with kitchen utensils hanging from its knob-like ears and a large mouth in front like an oven door.

Two hotplates lit up as the machine sniffed the steaming pies and cried, "After I have feasted on these substandard pies, I will eat you both for daring to deprive me of the original and best!" There was a whizzing noise as two arms with oven mitt hands shot out from slots on either side of the machine, grabbed up the pies

and crammed them into its mouth all at once.

"Cuthbert, did you hear that?" Arnold whimpered. "There'll be nothing left of us but c-c-crumbs!"

But Cuthbert was looking determinedly at the machine. "Now for the twist!" he mouthed to Arnold.

Mid-chew, the machine suddenly stopped guzzling. Its eyes turned a deeper red, its hotplate nostrils turned purple and steam began to seep out of its sides.

"NOT CUSTARD!" it roared. "CANNOT COMPUTE! CANNOT COMPUTE!" The machine frantically flailed its arms, sending boxes, bottles and rusty tools soaring through the air like missiles.

"Quick – grab an arm!" Cuthbert cried, as he narrowly missed getting a bolt through the neck.

Arnold waited for the arm to hurtle towards the ground before he seized hold of its oven mitt. "Ha ha!" he laughed triumphantly. "Got you!" But Arnold's flimsy frame couldn't hold the crazed arm down for long and soon he was thrown upwards.

"Keep holding on, Arnold!" Cuthbert yelled. Spotting a length of rope on the shelf, Cuthbert quickly pulled it down and tied a loop at one end. "Catch!" he cried

as he threw it
to Arnold.

As Arnold
reached out to catch
the rope, the machine's arm
gave a ferocious flap, nearly
throwing him off.

"Now loop it around the arm!"

"I can't!" Arnold wailed, tightening
his grip on the machine's arm.

"You can do it, Arnold!" Cuthbert
cried encouragingly.

Arnold was so dizzy that he saw three
arms instead of just one. Deciding the
middle one was most likely to be the real
thing, Arnold quickly hooked the rope

over the machine's oven mitt. Cuthbert pulled the other end as tightly as he could, bringing the arm under control. Sliding off, Arnold shrieked joyfully, "I did it! I did it!"

"Well done, Arnold! Now you hold the rope and I'll tackle the other arm!" Cuthbert grabbed the thrashing arm and pushed with all his might until it slid back inside the machine. Cuthbert then held the slot shut in case the arm remerged.

"How did you like your MUSTARD pies?" Cuthbert taunted the machine. "That's my secret ingredient – extra hot English mustard!" As he spoke, smoke began to pour out of the machine.

"TOO HOT!!!" it screeched, flames licking around its mouth.

Suddenly, Cuthbert became aware of a burning sensation in his fingers. He quickly pulled his hands away from the machine's boiling metal and blew on them. Before he realised his mistake, the machine's arm shot out of the slot and grabbed his left leg.

Suspended upside down, Cuthbert squeezed his eyes shut tight and yelled, "Run Arnold! Save yourself!"

The end
is pie

"Whisk the eggs with two fluid ounces of milk, one cucumber and a liberal helping of yam!" the machine screeched, bringing Cuthbert closer to its fiery mouth.

It's completely losing its marbles! Cuthbert thought, overcome with fear.

"Pat-a-cake, pat-a-cake, fat little pie man."

Cuthbert felt beads of sweat forming on his forehead.

"Doris, won't you come round to see me? We'll do a little dance and then eat a fat boy for tea!" it sang insanely.

The heat was unbearable. Cuthbert could smell his eyebrows beginning to singe as the flames licked ever closer to his head.

Then, all of a sudden, a strange chaotic music filled the shed. It sounded like a bird that had to fit its whole life's work into one song. A crazy bird at that! Cuthbert felt the machine loosen its grip slightly, then as the music grew faster it let go of Cuthbert's leg completely. Plummeting head first towards the ground, Cuthbert landed on something soft and squishy.

"Ouch!" it cried.

Cuthbert recognised that "ouch". It was Arnold!

"You came back!" Cuthbert yelled,

turning his friend the right way up.

"Of course I did!" Arnold said, adjusting his glasses.

As the music continued to flow, the flames withdrew into the machine's huge oven mouth. Wires sprung from its panels and smoke hissed from its sides.

"It's shutting down!" Arnold said with relief.

Smoke quickly filled the shed, making it impossible for them to see what was happening. Then... BANG!

"What was that?" Arnold squeaked.

Cuthbert didn't reply. Instead, he walked into the haze to find out. The machine had toppled over and was lying

on its side, flickering with what little life remained. As Cuthbert approached the wreckage, a shaking oven mitt reached out to him as the machine's mouth dropped open. Amid the crazed music and electrical sparks, a faint voice wheezed, "Were we so very different, you and I?"

Then the light from its bright red eyes faded and went out.

As the smoke cleared a little, Cuthbert looked around and was amazed to see Professor Ankles standing in the corner of the shed, busily thrashing a xylophone's keys with a pair of mallets.

"You can stop now, Dad!" Arnold cried.

"Sorry, I got a little absorbed," Professor Ankles said. He picked up Arnold and hugged him. "Thank goodness you boys are alright!"

"I hope you don't mind, Cuthbert, but I ran home to fetch Dad. I figured he might have something to do with this," Arnold said, looking at Professor Ankles for an explanation.

"Well, of course I didn't mean for this to happen, but yes — the machine is all my doing," Professor Ankles said, hanging his head with shame.

"How could you be so cruel to Granny?" Cuthbert shouted angrily.

"The machine wasn't supposed to demand food," Professor Ankles said. "It was supposed to *make* food! It was a surprise for Arnold that I've been working on for quite some time. My cooking is appalling and it isn't healthy to be eating take-away food all the time."

"So what went wrong?" Arnold asked his father.

"The machine was almost finished. I was typing nutritious meals into the machine's recipe chip when the sweet smell of custard pies came wafting in through an open window. They smelled so good I typed in 'custard pies'. It was then that the machine malfunctioned.

Sparks flew out of its sides and it began to rumble. Just as I was thinking 'back to the drawing board' the machine sprang to life, gave an almighty roar and flung me to the ground. I have no idea how long I was unconscious, but when I woke up the machine had fled! I turned the house upside down looking for it, and even thought I had found it when Cuthbert came round. But it was only the fridge."

"The smell of Granny's custard pies must have driven the machine over the edge," Cuthbert said sympathetically.

"Why didn't you tell someone, Dad?" Arnold groaned.

"I didn't want anyone to know that I can't cook," Professor Ankles said with embarrassment.

"His cooking *is* truly awful," Arnold whispered behind his hand to Cuthbert.

"Luckily, I had already installed a shut-down chip that responds to a particular sequence of notes when played on the xylophone. Hence my performance just now," Professor Ankles said, looking quite pleased with himself.

"What's going to happen to the machine now, Dad?"

"Well son, I think perhaps it's done enough damage." They turned to look at what remained of the machine. Cuthbert

couldn't help but feel a little sorry for it. After all, they shared an unwholesome appetite for Granny's custard pies.

"Then again," mused Professor Ankles, "as the great inventor Thomas Edison once said, 'Just because something doesn't do what you planned it to do doesn't mean it's useless.'"

Suddenly, the shed door flung open. Professor Ankles reached for his xylophone. They waited with bated breath. Then a pair of stockinged legs stepped into the murky shed.

"I'm sorry I'm so late! Please don't be angry with me!" croaked Granny. "I brought you a few extra custard pies to make up for it!" she cowered.

"It's OK, Granny!" Cuthbert called, stepping out of the smoke towards her. "You don't have to feed the machine any more!"

Granny was so surprised to see Cuthbert

that her dentures flew out of her mouth and across the shed.

"Cushbert," she rasped, "I'm sho shorry! It made me feed it your cushtard ties, shaid it would eat me if I made them for anyone elsh!"

"I'm the one who should be sorry, Granny," Cuthbert apologised. "I've been so greedy. I never appreciated all that cooking you did for me. Well, from now on things are going to change."

Two Weeks Later...

"They're here!"

Arnold bounded down the stairs two at a time. Pulling open the front door, he was met by Cuthbert and Granny, equipped with her trolley bag.

Once inside, Arnold led his guests into the steam-filled kitchen. "Ooh! I can't see a thing!" he said, waving his arms to clear the air.

"Dreadfully sorry, Master Arnold," a tinny voice replied. "I'll switch on my fan mechanism."

As the steam cleared they were greeted by a shiny metallic face. Gone were the glaring red eyes and the chomping jaws. In their place shone bright blue eyes and a wide, toothless smile. As an afterthought, Professor Ankles had given the machine a pink bow tie.

"Do take a seat, dinner is just ready," said Professor Ankles, wandering into the kitchen in his lab coat.

"Thank you," they chorused as they took their places at the dinner table.

"Oh, don't thank me, thank Edison," grinned the professor, gesturing to the machine.

After devouring several helpings of cream of cabbage soup, a pot of jellied eels, roast lamb with Yorkshire puddings and a variety of Swedish cheeses, Cuthbert opened Granny's trolley bag and pulled out four golden custard pies.

"And now for dessert," he said, proudly setting the pies on the table.

"Ooohh!" Professor Ankles and Arnold exclaimed.

"Cuthbert made them all by himself,

didn't you, Cuthy?" Granny boasted. "And he made me dinner last night so I didn't have to miss my favourite programme *Saving the Killer Badger Beasts*."

"My smell sensor indicates something delicious," came Edison's voice from the other side of the room.

"Don't worry, Edison," Cuthbert said, "We'll save some for you!" But he quickly gobbled up *his* last piece – just to be on the safe side.